To Lynne and Peter, who were the originals — A. B.
To my father, with love — J. T.

Viking Kestrel
Penguin Books Australia Ltd, 487 Maroondah Highway, P.O. Box 257 Ringwood,
Victoria 3134, Australia
Penguin Books (N.Z.) Ltd, 182–190 Wairau Road, Auckland 10, New Zealand
Penguin Books Ltd, Harmondsworth, Middlesex, England
Penguin Books Canada Ltd, 2801 John Street, Markham, Ontario, Canada L3R 1B4

First published by Viking Kestrel, 1988

10 9 8 7 6 5 4 3 2

Produced by Viking O'Neil
56 Claremont Street, South Yarra, Victoria 3141, Australia
A division of Penguin Books Australia Ltd

Printed in Hong Kong through Bookbuilders

National Library of Australia
Cataloguing-in-Publication data

Baillie, Allan, 1943–
    Drac and the gremlin

    ISBN 0 670 82271 X

    I. Tanner, Jane. II. Title.

A823'.3

DRAC
and the
GREMLIN

Allan Baillie

pictures by
Jane Tanner

VIKING KESTREL

Shhh! Quiet...
Drac, the Warrior Queen of Tirnol Two, is in terrible danger.
She is fearless, as fast as the whirlwind,
as wise as the White Wizard ...

Drac must capture the Gremlin of the Groaning Grotto.
She knows he is quick, quiet as a spider,
and very, very dangerous.
She must be _so_ careful...

'Aaaargh!'

Drac fights off the Gremlin's treacherous attack
with her ultra-laser beam.

She chases him into the quivering jungles,
across the bubbling seas, and through the dark
and poisonous fumes of the black volcano.

At last Drac traps the Gremlin in the misty valleys of Melachon.

At that moment,
an emerald eaglon
slips from the sky,
bringing a fearful message
from the Mountain
of the White Wizard.

'Great Queen Drac, come to my aid before all is lost!

'I am being attacked by General Min and her
Hissing Horde and you are the planet's only hope.
But beware the Terrible Tongued Dragon...'

Drac thinks for a second. Then she shakes
the panting Gremlin: 'We must unite against this awful peril.
You will join me and we will save Tirnol Two!'

'Gerroff!' says the Gremlin gallantly.

Drac and the Gremlin leap aboard her Anti-Gravity
Solar-Powered Planet Hopper. They sweep through the clouds
to the Mountain of the White Wizard.

They land deep in the jungle and creep up on General
Min, furtive as a fly.

'Shhh . . .' breathes Drac. 'We will ambush her.'

'Shurrup,' says the Gremlin.

They have arrived just in time.
The White Wizard is transforming into a silver flutterwing
and is preparing to escape.
But General Min has seen the change.
She is about to pounce.

'Gotcha!'
Drac and the Gremlin spring before General Min can attack.

The General is caught by surprise.
With a howl of despair she flees deep into the jungle.

But the White Wizard hovers near Drac.

'There is still more danger!'
she whispers softly. 'More danger ...'

Drac hears the trees of the jungle
shake behind her ...

the Terrible Tongued Dragon is upon them!

Drac speeds through the jungle, but she can feel the fire from the Dragon's mouth.

She turns to fight.

But the Dragon is too big, too fierce.

The terrible tongue is poised to destroy her.

But all is not lost.
The Gremlin mounts his Supersonic Jetbike
and roars into attack with micron-blasters blazing.

'Get him!' says Drac.

'Brummn!' says the Gremlin, fiercely.

Together they drive the Terrible Tongued Dragon from the Mountain.

Later they return to the palace.

'You have saved the planet' says the White Wizard. 'We are very grateful. Please accept as your reward our highest honour, the Twin Crimson Cones of Tirnol Two.'

Drac the Warrior Queen and the crafty Gremlin
leave the palace of the White Wizard
for their secret jungle hideout ...

always on the alert for their next perilous mission.